ATHENEUM BOOKS
BY JAMES HOWE

Bunnicula
(with Deborah Howe)

Teddy Bear's Scrapbook
(with Deborah Howe)

Howliday Inn

A Night Without Stars

The Celery Stalks at Midnight

Morgan's Zoo

There's a Monster Under My Bed

What Eric Knew

Stage Fright

Eat Your Poison, Dear

Nighty-Nightmare

Pinky and Rex

Pinky and Rex Get Married

Dew Drop Dead

Pinky and Rex and the Mean Old Witch

Pinky and Rex and the Spelling Bee

PINKY and REX
and the
Spelling Bee

by James Howe
illustrated by Melissa Sweet

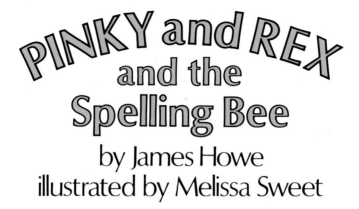

ATHENEUM   **1991**   **NEW YORK**

Collier Macmillan Canada
TORONTO

Maxwell Macmillan International Publishing Group
NEW YORK OXFORD SINGAPORE SYDNEY

Text copyright © 1991 by James Howe
Illustrations copyright © 1991 by Melissa Sweet

Atheneum
Macmillan Publishing Company
866 Third Avenue, New York, NY 10022

Collier Macmillan Canada, Inc.
1200 Eglinton Avenue East
Suite 200
Don Mills, Ontario M3C 3N1
First Edition

Printed in Hong Kong by South China Printing Company (1988) Ltd.
10 9 8 7 6 5 4 3 2 1

Library of Congress Cataloging-in-Publication Data
Howe, James.
Pinky and Rex and the spelling bee/by James Howe; illustrated
by Melissa Sweet. p. cm.
Summary: Excited about holding on to his position as the best
speller in the second grade, Pinky has an embarrassing accident but
is cheered up by his best friend, Rex.
ISBN 0-689-31618-6
[1. Contests—Fiction. 2 Schools—Fiction. 3. Friendship—
Fiction.] I. Sweet, Melissa, ill. II. Title.
PZ7.H83727Ps 1991 [E]—dc20
89-78305 CIP AC

To Zoe, who loved words
even before she could spell

—J. H.

To Mimi, Bob, Becky, and Charlie

—M. S.

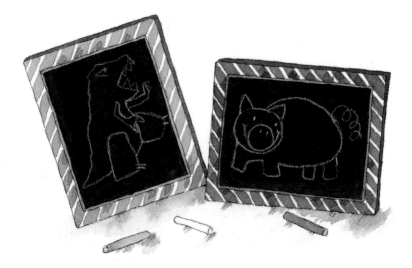

Contents

Chapter 1

The Big Day

Pinky could hardly believe it. The big day had arrived at last.

"Slow down," Rex said. "Why are you walking so fast?"

"I can't wait to get to school," said Pinky. "I've been getting ready all week."

Rex stopped walking. "Getting ready for what?" she asked. She didn't remember anything about there being a test that day.

"The spelling bee," said Pinky. "I *love* spelling bees."

"Oh, no!" Rex cried. "I forgot all about it. I *hate* spelling bees. Do you think my mother would believe me if I told her I got sick on the way to school and had to come home?"

Pinky shook his head.

Rex dropped to the ground and rested her chin on both hands. She did not look happy.

"Come on," Pinky said, picking up Rex's fallen book bag, "you can't stay here all day. Besides, you'll do all right."

Rex sighed. "Pinky, you're my best friend. You're not supposed to lie to me. You know I'm terrible at spelling. I'm *not* going to do all right."

Sitting down next to Rex, Pinky said, "So what if you're not good at spelling? It doesn't matter."

"That's easy for you to say," said Rex. "You're not going to make a fool of yourself. I *hate* looking stupid. It's bad enough to make mistakes when you're all by yourself. But when you have to stand up in front of the whole class… I just know everyone is going to laugh at me, Pinky. They'll laugh and they'll say, 'That Rex is *so* stupid.'"

"I won't laugh at you," Pinky told Rex. "And I won't think you're stupid, either."

"You're just saying that because you know you're smarter than I am."

"Maybe in some things I am," said Pinky. "But you're smarter in other things. Like games. And you know lots more about dinosaurs than I do. You even know how to spell all their names."

This made Rex feel a little better. "Maybe you're right," she said. "But I'll tell you one thing. If everybody laughs at me, I'm moving to the moon."

Chapter 2

The Champion Speller of the Whole Second Grade

Spelling was one thing Pinky knew he did better than anyone. He had never made a mistake. Not ever. Not on a test. Not in a spelling bee. He was the champion speller of the whole second grade. Sometimes this made Pinky nervous, but it made him feel special, too.

He was so excited when the spelling bee began that he almost forgot how much Rex was dreading it. But then the teacher called Rex's name, and he saw the look on her face. He wished there were some way he could help his friend.

"Pencil," Rex repeated after the teacher. Pinky noticed Rex's cheeks getting red. "Uh, pencil... p–e–n–c–l–e. Pencil."

Some of the boys and girls began to snicker. "Stop that," said Ms. Hernandez. "There's nothing funny about making a mistake. That was a good try, Rex. Better luck next time."

"There won't be a next time," Rex muttered, as she passed Pinky on the way back to her seat. "I'm moving to the moon right after school."

"Pinky," said Ms. Hernandez.
"Would you please spell *robin*?"

That's easy, Pinky thought. She
must be saving the tough ones for
later. "Robin," he repeated.
"R–o–b–i–n. Robin."

"Very good," Ms. Hernandez
said. Pinky noticed the special way
she smiled at him.

After twenty minutes, there were only six children left in the spelling bee. Pinky looked up and down the line. He wasn't worried about Tanya or Marci or Trevor or Ben. They were good spellers, but they weren't *great* spellers. However, at the far end of the line was a new boy, named Anthony.

He had been in Pinky's class for only a couple of weeks. Pinky hadn't thought he was all that smart, but now he began to wonder. Ms. Hernandez had given Anthony some pretty tough words. And Anthony had spelled each one correctly right away. Pinky was beginning to worry.

"Lunch," he heard Ms. Hernandez say.

"Lunch," said Pinky. "L–u–n–c–h. Lunch."

He heard the class laughing. Had he spelled it wrong? Ms. Hernandez was laughing, too.

"No, Pinky," the teacher said, giving Pinky that special smile again. "I meant that it's time for lunch. We'll continue the spelling bee when we get back from the cafeteria."

Chapter 3

Nervous Pinky

The cafeteria was the noisiest room in the school. But even with all the first graders and all the second graders eating and talking and laughing at the same time, Pinky hardly heard a thing.

"Earth to Pinky," said Rex.

"Huh?" Pinky looked up.

"You haven't eaten anything," Rex pointed out. "Aren't you hungry?"

Pinky shook his head. His peanut butter sandwich was untouched. He hadn't even opened his bag of potato chips. All he'd had for lunch were three cartons of milk and two glasses of juice. Being nervous made Pinky very thirsty.

"If you're not going to eat that sandwich," he heard someone say, "I'll take it. My mom packed—yuck—cold meat loaf." Trevor was leaning halfway across the table.

"Here," said Pinky. "You can have the potato chips, too."

"Cool," Trevor said.

"Are you worried about the spelling bee?" Rex asked.

Pinky nodded. "Maybe a little," he admitted. "It's that new kid, Anthony. What if he beats me, Rex?"

"So what if he does?" said Rex, with a shrug. "You know what you told me: 'It doesn't matter.'"

"But everyone will laugh at me. And I won't be the champion speller of the whole second grade anymore."

"Everyone laughed at me," Rex said. "I got over it, didn't I? Besides, I'll still be your friend even if you're not the champion speller."

Pinky gave Rex a weak smile. "I know that," he said. "But I *really* want to win. If I lose that spelling bee, it will be the worst thing that ever happened to me."

"I can think of lots of worse things than losing a spelling bee," said Rex.

But Pinky wasn't listening. He was on his way back to the cafeteria line for another carton of milk.

Chapter 4

The Worst Thing
That Ever Happened

"*Suppose,*" said Ms. Hernandez.

"Suppose," Marci repeated. She looked over at the door. Pinky felt sure she was going to make a mistake. It was ten minutes since the second half of the spelling bee had begun. There were only three spellers left.

"Marci?" the teacher said.

"Uh, suppose," said Marci. "S–u–p . . . o–s–e. Suppose."

"I'm sorry, Marci," Ms. Hernandez said. She turned to Pinky. Pinky glanced to his left. Anthony was smiling.

"Suppose," said Pinky. "S–u–p–p–o–s–e. Suppose."

"Very good. Anthony, will you spell *vacation*, please?"

Pinky couldn't watch. He knew Anthony was going to get it right. He swallowed and told himself to breathe slowly.

"*Second,*" he heard Ms. Hernandez say, after Anthony had correctly spelled his word.

Pinky saw Rex watching him. She smiled, as if to tell him, "You can do it." He was no longer so sure. He'd studied that word just this morning, but now he had a hard time picturing it in his mind.

"Second. S...e...c...um."

"Yes?" said Ms. Hernandez. She gave him the same you-can-do-it look that Rex had a moment earlier.

"S–e–c...o...n...d. Second."

Some of the kids cheered. Pinky felt himself start to relax. Maybe he *would* win, after all.

Anthony almost stumbled over *spinach*. Pinky began to think, I'm going to do it. I'm going to win. I'll still be the champ!

Five minutes went by. The class-
room had grown very quiet. "My
goodness," said Ms. Hernandez. "I
can't seem to find words that are
hard enough for the two of you.
Maybe we should declare a tie."

"No!" the class cried. Pinky and
Anthony shook their heads. They
both wanted to win. Pinky was
beginning to wish that the spelling
bee would end soon, though. He
had forgotten to go to the bathroom
before returning to class after lunch.
Now he was feeling all that milk and
juice he had had to drink. One more
round, he told himself. I'll beat him
in the next round, and then after we
sit down, I'll raise my hand and ask
to go to the bathroom.

Five more minutes passed. Pinky pressed his legs together and was starting to feel as if his head was going to float away. He had to go to the bathroom *very* badly. But he couldn't leave now. He had to win first, he just had to.

Each time that it was Anthony's turn, Pinky thought: Mess up, Anthony. Get it wrong.

But Anthony never made a mistake. And then it happened.

"Anthony, will you please spell *excuse?*" said Ms. Hernandez.

"Excuse," Anthony repeated. For the first time, a look of doubt crossed his face. "E–x...u–s–e."

Pinky couldn't believe it. Anthony had spelled the word

wrong. All Pinky had to do now was get it right, and he would still be the champion speller of the whole second grade. He was so excited he could hardly stand it.

"Excuse," he said, without even waiting for Ms. Hernandez to call his name. "E–x–c–u–s–e. Excuse."

The class cheered. Ms. Hernandez was smiling. So was Rex. Pinky let out a big sigh of relief. And then he had the strangest feeling. Something warm and wet was running down his leg. The class stopped cheering. They began to laugh instead.

Pinky looked in horror at the puddle on the floor.

Chapter 5

Laughter

Pinky wanted to run out of the room. But all he could do was stand there, in front of his whole laughing class, and feel like a fool. How could this have happened? He wasn't a *baby*.

He looked over at Anthony. The new kid was doubled over with laughter, as if he didn't even care that he'd just lost a spelling bee.

The truth was, Pinky no longer
cared that he had *won*. Rex had
been right. There *were* worse things
than losing.

Ms. Hernandez waited patiently for the laughter to die down. "All right, boys and girls," she said, "that's enough. I think we've gotten the giggles out of our system now."

"Pinky peed!" someone shouted, making everyone burst out laughing all over again.

The teacher came over to Pinky and Anthony. "Sit down," she said softly to Anthony. Then to Pinky, she whispered, "These things happen, Pinky. I know it's hard not to be

embarrassed, but it isn't the end of the world. I'll get some paper towels. Do you have a pair of gym pants with you?"

Pinky nodded.

"Let's quiet down, everyone," Ms. Hernandez said, turning back to the class. "Ben, would you go with Pinky to the bathroom so he can change his pants? And I see no reason for any more laughter. I know it seemed funny to you that Pinky wet his pants, but he was very excited about winning the spelling bee and had an accident. That's all. I'm sure every one of you has been so nervous or excited at one time or another that you suddenly had to pee very badly."

"Ms. Hernandez said *pee*," Trevor whispered. Some of the boys laughed into their hands.

"Maybe you were luckier than Pinky and made it to the bathroom in time, but the same thing could have happened to you. Here's something else to think about: Pinky is still the champion. Good work, Pinky."

Pinky looked up to see Ms. Hernandez giving him that smile of hers. But it didn't make him feel special this time. All he felt was something stinging his eyes. When he realized what it was, he ran out of the room before he made even more of a fool of himself by letting everyone see him cry.

Chapter 6

The Long Walk Home

Most of the time, Pinky was more of a talker than Rex. But today Rex chattered the whole way home. She talked about what she hoped she was going to have for dinner that night and about the dinosaur puzzle her uncle and aunt had sent her that had over seven hundred pieces and about a TV commercial she'd seen with a singing dog and she couldn't figure out how they did it because it really looked as if the dog could sing. She never mentioned anything about lunch or the new kid, Anthony, or Ms. Hernandez. And she made extra sure she didn't say a word about spelling bees.

Pinky wasn't really listening. He just nodded his head and kept his eyes on his feet as they moved slowly along. Rex was his best friend, but today he wished he was walking home alone. He wondered what he would tell his parents. He wondered how he would ever dare go to school again. And then he thought about Amanda. Just knowing how his little sister would tease him and tell *every-body* made his stomach hurt.

Then he heard Rex ask, "So, you want to go with me to the moon?"

He knew she was trying to make him laugh, but he didn't even smile.

"Let's see," said Rex. "What should we take? All your animals, of course, and all my dinosaurs. And

we'll need food. You bring peanut
butter. I'll bring ice pops. Do you
like ice pops?"

"You know I do," Pinky
muttered.

"Good. Do you think we should
take raspberry ice pops or lemon-
lime ice pops?" When Pinky didn't
answer, she said, "Maybe we should
take both."

"Don't be stupid," said Pinky.
"Ice pops will melt before we get to
the moon."

"Oh, yeah. I guess I *am* stupid."

Pinky looked at Rex. "No, you're not," he said. "I didn't mean it like that."

"Maybe I am sometimes," she said.

"Yeah, and maybe I'm a baby sometimes."

"I don't think you are. And you know what, Pinky? I didn't laugh at you today. I felt bad when that happened." Pinky looked at Rex, then quickly turned away.

After walking a little way in silence, Rex bent down and picked up two small stones. One was white, the other was gray with spots. They were both almost perfectly round.

"These are friendship stones," she declared. "Hold out your hand."

Pinky held out his hand, and Rex placed the white stone in it. "Okay, repeat after me. As long as I keep this stone..."

"As long as I keep this stone," said Pinky.

"I will never think you're stupid."

"I will never think you're stupid."

"And I will never laugh at you, even if all the other kids are laughing."

Pinky closed his hand tightly
over the white stone. "I will never
laugh at you even if the other kids
laugh," he said.

"Because you're my friend," Rex
said.

"Because you're my friend,"
said Pinky.

"Hey, Pinky, why are you
wearing your gym pants?"

Pinky and Rex looked up to see Pinky's little sister, Amanda, running toward them.

Before Pinky could think of anything to say, Rex answered for him. "Because," she said, "Pinky is the champion speller of the whole second grade. And Ms. Hernandez said only the champion speller gets to wear his gym pants for the whole day."

"Wow," said Amanda. "Race you."

Pinky and Rex and Amanda ran the rest of the way home. For the first time ever, Pinky and Rex let Amanda win.